A Tin

Lost Trinket Series Book 1

Sherrie Lea Morgan

A Timed Wager, Lost Trinket Series Book 1© 2016

Sherrie Lea Morgan

Editor: Lindsey Loucks
Cover: Yocla Designs

Dedication

This book is dedicated to my twin Jerrie Lynn. Words have always been unnecessary between us. This time, though, it is important enough to write them. Thank you for being my sister, my twin, my best friend and supporting me forever and always.

psychometry (sī'kämətrē) *noun*

1. the ability to discover facts about an event or person by touching inanimate objects associated with them.

Chapter One

*I*s that blood?

Bent over, I focused on the dark stain on Mr. Lawrence's carpet. Did some other client get worse news than me and they actually bled during their meeting?

"Shannon, stop that and sit up. He's about to come around to check on you," Stephanie said.

"Leave me alone," I whispered and straightened to face Mr. Lawrence's scowl. I'd seen that disappointment-laced image once before when he faced a crying woman in his office several years ago. I tucked a loose strand of hair behind my ear and leaned forward, ignoring the blast of cigar residue he exuded. "Mr. Lawrence, are you sure Grandma Brenda would want this?" *Of course she would. It was in her will, wasn't it? Why? Why would she do this?* "I didn't even know she had a sister."

"Ms. Pryce." Mr. Lawrence's nasally voice sharpened. "I am the executor only. All the decisions have been made. However, if you wish to contest it, you

1

get nothing. It is all outlined in the will…as I've explained."

I rose, ignoring the way my shirt clung to my back. This guy obviously didn't believe in using air conditioning. "No, I won't contest it. I only wish there were more explanations. It's only been a month since she passed. Are you sure she didn't leave me a letter or anything?" I had to ask. I couldn't help myself.

"If she had, I'd have given it to you." He stood and handed me the large envelope with my copy of the paperwork he'd already read to me.

"So, I only have until—" I checked the paper in my hand. "6:00 p.m. on Friday to pack up and get out?" Bile roiled inside me, and dizziness threatened the edges of my brain.

"The school has workers planned this weekend to get the place ready for student admissions starting Monday."

Wait a minute. "Monday? How can they plan that fast?"

Mr. Lawrence winced.

Yeah, right. "They knew the moment she died they'd get our home—"

"Your grandmother's home, not yours," he reminded me.

"Well, not anymore. Doesn't matter that I've lived there half my life. It was ours." *Jerk.*

Mr. Lawrence handed me another large envelope. "It was also my understanding that you'd already begun packing with plans to move out. In here is the deed to your great aunt's store, along with the keys. Good luck and I'll have Trisha walk you out. I've got another appointment in five minutes."

Trisha held out her hand as if to grab my arm if I refused to leave. As if I'd give him the satisfaction. I glared once at Mr. Lawrence, spun on my heels, and followed Trisha out. After signing the documents in silence, I slunk out of the attorney's office and headed to my car.

"That bites, Shan," Stephanie said.

My head throbbed, and the buzzing returned. The long awaited bright sun of spring decided to glare in my eyes. Tears pooled then fell down my cheeks. I slapped a hand on my chest when my heart raced and pounded against my ribs. *What am I going to do?*

"Shannon, listen. This is a good thing."

I froze then turned toward her. "A good thing? Really?"

Steph scanned the street and sidewalk. "You sure you want to talk directly to me out here? It's not like we're alone."

"I don't care. Everyone thinks I'm crazy anyway, right?" My hands flapped around like wild fish swimming upstream as my voice pitched higher. "I have less than three days to pack the rest of my belongings and go where? Do what? Live on the streets?"

"Aren't you supposed to breathe about now? I bet if you ground yourself, you'll feel better."

"I don't want to." *Damn, I sound like a kid.* "Just give me a minute," I requested through clenched teeth. When Stephanie opened her mouth, I raised my finger. "Just one minute alone. Please."

Stephanie nodded and her glowing shape evaporated. Shoulders dropped, I blinked to clear my eyes. I located, got in, and cranked the engine to my beloved five-year-old slate grey Scion. Resting my head on the steering wheel, I closed my eyes. *Inhale. Exhale.* The air conditioner blew cold air across my face.

A Timed Wager: Lost Trinket Series Book 1

Grandma Brenda had a sister named Caroline, whom she'd never told me about. Now, I owned Great Aunt Caroline's antique shop outside of Augusta in some dinky town called Petrie's Crossing. Why was Steph the only ghost I saw? If I could see Grandma, I could ask her what the hell was going on. I could ask her why she did this. I swallowed past the lump in my throat and shuddered. I couldn't though. She'd left me like my parents left me.

"Okay, times up," Steph said from the passenger seat. "Listen, you're only twenty-six. Lots of people start a new life at that age. Besides, you already planned to leave. This has only pushed you ahead by a few weeks is all. No one in this Petrie's Crossing will have heard of you or what you've done. You wanted a fresh start, so here you are. Suck it up, and let's see where this path leads you."

As usual, she was right in so many ways. Grandma was gone, someone leaked my name to the newspaper, and people went crazy wanting to hire me to find their missing relatives. I couldn't do that anymore. I rolled my shoulders and grunted.

"Steph, I've lost my home." Nothing like stating the obvious to a dead person.

"You know, if that's an older town like Augusta, I bet it has living spaces above the shops. If you own that building the store is in, you'll have a place to live. Since your closed down your online work, your bank account isn't going to grow on its own."

"You know why I closed it." I faced her. "This is an antique store. Those things are hit and miss with my ability. I'll have to wear my gloves all the time to avoid unwanted visions."

"True, but since it's been empty for who knows how long, you'd have to wear gloves anyway to get it cleaned up," she said. "Besides, you've been working on focusing your gift for a couple years now. It's been a year since that incident with the newspaper. You can handle this."

"Great, new home and lots of cleaning involved. I can't wait."

"It'll work out, Shan. I feel it in my bones." She flipped her long blonde hair over her shoulder and grinned.

"You don't have bones. You're mainly mist," I pointed out, strapping the seatbelt on.

"Yes, well. You know what I mean… And stop being a baby about this," she demanded.

6

I sighed. "Fine. You're right. I guess the time to start over has arrived." I pulled out of the parking space and headed home. "Good thing I'm not a hoarder."

Steph laughed. "This is a great opportunity. I know it. I'll be right along with you, and you won't have to do this alone."

I didn't bother to ask why she was always with me. I'd gone down that path before, and she'd never given me an answer that made any sense. Comfort battled with guilt, though, every time she showed up.

Chapter Two

"Turn here. There should be a parking area in the back," Steph mumbled in the confines of my car. The shadowy street loomed in front of me, lighted on each corner by what could have been gas lamps at one time.

"Yep, I know." *For the umpteenth time.* "But I want to check out the front first. See what it looks like."

After pulling the car near the curb, I parked and got out. The meter had expired, but since it was eleven at night, no one should be monitoring it. I checked out the street, and it was empty as far as I could see. I stood in front of Aunt Caroline's—no, *my*—store. The brick storefront glared back at me with two large dirt-stained windows. The cracked and peeling paint on the wooden door proved it had been vacant for years. Jutting above the door, a rusting metal arm barely held on to a small wooden sign with broken chains. *Trinkets,* the sign read.

What had I gotten myself…? *I'm not going there again.* Sighing, I shook my head and headed back to the car where Steph waited.

"How come you didn't come with me?" I asked.

"For what? I don't do exteriors. Let's get inside."

"Fine," I mumbled and took the car around the corner to the back street.

"Dang, it's dark back here. Don't these people believe in streetlights?"

"There's streetlights in the front all along the road."

"I know. It's behind these buildings that's irritating." Ten miles an hour and I still couldn't see but a few feet in front of me. "Why's it so foggy?"

"I don't know. Maybe we're close to water?"

"Augusta has a river near it, so maybe it meanders around here too? There it is." I pulled into the space marked number seven. Grabbing my overnight bag and the keys from Mr. Lawrence's envelope, I slammed the car door and headed toward my new home.

"Well, well. What have we here?" a sleazy voice whispered out of the dark.

Shit. Pepper spray, where's the pepper spray? I dropped my keys inside my purse and plunged into the depths,

9

searching. I shifted to put my back toward the door and peered in the direction of the voice. An equally sleazy man who'd eaten way too many fast food meals sauntered toward me from my right.

I wrapped my fingers around the spray and whipped it out. The man held his hands in front of him. He looked to be in his early thirties, but I wasn't sure.

"Whoa now, lady. I'm not here to hurt you." He walked closer, and although wrinkled, his clothes were clean.

"Stay back," I warned. "I've got pepper spray."

Where's my phone? I need the cops. I need a gun. No, what I need is to be home and not in this dinky little town west of Augusta, existing with its dilapidated buildings and empty streets…and sleazy men who creep around back roads.

"Listen, I only came here to introduce myself. My name is Bobby Green. I own that there pawnshop two doors down. I heard you drive around and thought I'd see what was what."

I scanned his face. The loose skin around his eyes jiggled when he talked. But he hadn't moved. I peeked behind him, and an old blue Buick sat parked two buildings away. There was a light at the back door gleaming a dusty yellow across the hood of the car. I nodded and lowered the can, but my fingers kept their grip. Just in case.

"I'm Shannon. I'm the new owner of Trinkets."

"Oh, you are, are you?" He chuckled and took a step.

Automatically, my hand rose, gripping the spray can tight. He stepped back. *Well, he's not stupid. Gotta give him that much.* I tilted my head. "Is there a problem with that?"

"Oh no. It's great that you're here. Getting that building cleaned will definitely bring in some business. I'm surprised it took this long."

"Took this long for what?" I asked.

"The neighborhood filed another complaint with the town council just last week. Trinkets is an eye sore. Another month and the council promised to start the paperwork to fine the owner." He grinned. "I'm glad someone is here to finally take care of it. And if that someone happens to be a pretty little thing like yourself, even better." He rubbed his hands together, and I fought to not roll my eyes. "Since you're new and all, why don't I buy you breakfast tomorrow? Welcome you to the town and all."

I shook my head. "Thank you, but I'm not sure if this place is even livable right now. I'm only here to check it out tonight."

"You need a place to stay? I've got an extra room at my place."

His wink made my stomach cringe. I doubt I'd get much sleep at his place. "Thank you, but no. I'm fine." I tossed the spray in my bag, grabbed the keys, and jammed them in the back door of Trinkets. "Good night." I rushed inside, spun around, and relocked the door.

Inhale. Exhale.

I slid my hand on the wall near the doorknob. I'd called and arranged the utilities to be turned back on starting today. My finger caught the switch, and I flipped it. One then two lights popped, and with a loud hum, the fluorescent light above the door shot a dim glow over me. I turned. I stood in what seemed like a back storage space with a small hallway leading to the front of the store. To my left, stairs leading up appeared to be sturdy even though covered in a dingy yellow rose runner. Okay, flowers were pretty.

Clean or not, I couldn't afford a hotel room. I stepped forward and reached for the banister.

Chapter Three

"First things first. Storefront in the morning. Sleep tonight," I whispered while mounting the stairs. Each step creaked ominously into the darkness. Silence filled the air along with an odor of dust.

"It's really dingy on this floor," Steph called from the top of the steps. "I checked it out, and there's no one alive or dead up here."

"Oh, hey thanks," I yelled. "I was really worried about that."

"Hey, just sayin'. No need to be snippy."

"Whatever. I'm only interested in sleeping tonight. I'll deal with everything else tomorrow."

"The bed's not made. But it looks like Aunt Caroline expected it to be a while before someone moved in. There's what looks like clean linens in some of those vacuum-packed bags on the bed."

"Good. Pillows?" I asked, following her down the hall.

Steph evaporated and her voice came from the room at the end. "Yep, pillows, too, and a really pretty quilt. Looks handmade."

"Awesome." I rounded the corner and stopped short.

The bedroom held three pieces of furniture. The king-size four-poster bed had its back against the front of the building. An old rocking chair sat in the corner, and a large bureau loomed beside it. All the pieces had drop cloths lying on the floor nearby.

"You took off the covers, I hope."

"I can help with small stuff," she said with a grin. "All you have to do is make the bed and crash. The sun should come right in those front windows, so you don't need an alarm anymore." She waved off to the left where a small door stood open. "That's the master bath, and it's clean enough. Looks like it's supplied too."

"We'll see how much sun can get through that dirt." No cobwebs hung in the corners, and the floor had minimal dust. "That's weird."

"Weird? What?" Steph asked.

"How come there's no cobwebs here? And the floor looks like the place has been empty for only a few weeks,

15

not years." I spun around. "And you said the bathroom was clean."

Steph shrugged. "I don't know. Are you going to complain or sleep?"

"I'm not complaining, just making an observation. What's the rush?" I asked.

"Nothing. Just wanted to be sure you get rested so you're not a grouch in the morning."

I shooed her. "Go do your thing or whatever. I'm crashing now."

I popped the seal of the bag holding the quilt and pillow. As soon as it aired up, I unzipped it and pulled the items out. A quick sniff confirmed their freshness. Dropping on the bed, I kicked off my sandals, wrapped the quilt around me, and let my head drop on the feather-filled pillow. My eyes closed, and the odor of lemons wafting around me was my last thought before my mind shut down.

****

A clattering sound, echoing from outside, startled me awake. I squinted into the darkness surrounding me. Nothing. I waited, and another clattering noise followed by a scratching made me scramble to the edge.

16

What is that? I held my breath. Another scratch resounded in the dark.

I released my breath then slipped on my sandals, grabbed my phone, and slowly worked my way out of the room. I kept the lights off and headed down the hall. I paused at the top of the stairs. Something scratched at the back door. I waited. When the mewling started, I knew. A cat...or kitten wanted in. I stood by the back door and listened. The mewling continued. *Crud.*

"Steph, you around?" I whispered.

Silence. Only the plaintive cat sounds greeted me. The crying grew louder. *Oh man.* I unlocked and opened the back door a few inches. It was enough. The orange kitten slipped in and started winding itself around my ankles. I peered outside and then back at the little feline.

"Where's your mommy, little one?"

The kitten couldn't be very old. It was smaller than my size seven foot that now became the recipient of the kitten's patty-caking. Sighing, I checked again outside. No meowing mama missing her kitten. No movement at all. *Great.*

"Ouch." I gasped when a kitten claw dug into the inside of my little toe. I bent and picked it up. Its mewling grew louder when it nipped at my fingers. "I can't feed you. I have nothing here." An image of my water bottle upstairs flashed in my head. The kitten's cries pulled on my heartstrings. *Poor thing.* I tucked it in my side, and after latching the back door, headed upstairs once again.

I opened one door, then another. Finally, I located a little kitchenette area and searched the cabinets until I found a small plastic bowl and rinsed it out. Milk would be better, but water was all I had tonight. Taking the kitten with me, I returned to my room, pulled out the bottle from my bag, and poured water in the bowl on the floor. The kitten lapped it up, and I shook my head. That wasn't going to last long. Digging into my purse, I grabbed my phone and checked the time. Four o'clock in the morning. No one would be awake, and I had no idea where the nearest grocery store was located. The sign on the corner drugstore had said the owner wouldn't return for another three weeks.

The kitten weaved around my ankles again, and its bowl was empty. I picked it up, peeked at its underside, and grinned. A girl kitty. I lay back down, and after tucking the quilt around both of us, the kitten snuggled against my neck. I closed my eyes, listening to soft purrs.

Then I wondered if anyone else had a key to this place.

Chapter Four

My eyes opened to a set of small blue ones staring at me. I jerked back before realizing it was the kitten. She scampered across the blue toned Bargello quilt and jumped to the floor, then ran out the door. Her nails clicked along the hallway. I shrugged then stretched. The morning sunrise filtered in and shot small streams of light onto the walls. If I hung some crystals near the windows, the color prisms would be beautiful in the morning hours.

I grabbed my phone to check my email. I doubted there would be much call for psychometry in this small town. Likely they considered it to be something for wackos only. The business I gained from the local metaphysical shops back in Birmingham worked in getting a nice savings account balance. But could I keep that type of business going hours away? Maybe. If I was willing to lower my prices to compensate for shipping costs. The amount of my savings I'd deplete with this store was another matter altogether. Did I even want to dump money in this place? It wasn't like I had any other place to live, but running an antique store?

Questions with no answers…just like the rest of my life.

After tossing the phone in my bag, I made the bed up, located a broom, and swept the floors. Not much dust, but enough. I located a linen closet filled with more vacuum-packed bags. Inside the four I opened, all the sheets and towels smelled clean. After emptying my travel bag, I grabbed a shower, dressed, and tried to stop the rapid ripples of nerves threatening to take over. *Routine actions and regular breathing.*

I stepped over to the window and scanned the area. A meter maid strolled along the front street. Did they call them meter maids still? Did it matter? Officer might be better. Near the pawnshop sat several empty cars, and a delivery truck rounded the corner to go behind the Italian diner across the street. At least the diner had a corner spot. Did it make a difference here? Did it serve breakfast? That was more important now since my stomach growled its need in the barren room.

Food. Groceries. I inspected the kitchenette. Okay, flipping on the light and taking stock, not a kitchenette. A full kitchen. The hum of the refrigerator indicated it was working. I opened the door and popped my head in. No weird odors. It'd been scrubbed clean. Good in a weird way. Gas stove. Old with a small layer of dust, it still clicked and lit when I turned the knob. No dishwasher. *Well, can't have everything.*

My stomach bellowed out its need again. Food first, then time to clean up. I went back and grabbed the shop keys and my purse. Heading down the stairway, I searched around the bottom floor, avoiding the dust-covered displays of antiques, boxes of knick-knacks, and long wooden shelves of more items. The absence of any drop cloths allowed dust to settle in the crevices. I frowned. The place shouted garage sale more than antique shop.

At least it stayed cool on the main level. The bricks likely helped with that. I glanced around. Those dust-filled fans would not be turned on until I could get them cleaned. Face masks and gloves. I might as well buy a painter's suit. *Drat.*

"Here kitty, kitty, kitty," I called out.

Silence greeted me and I shrugged. Well, she had to be here somewhere. I went out the front door and turned again to inspect the store facing. Oh man, it was worse in the sunlight. Looking up and down the street, the rest of the buildings displayed different degrees of decent to good condition. I'd file a complaint too. Trinkets stood out like an unwanted stepchild.

"You can fix that," Steph whispered in my ear.

Her cold presence caused goosebumps to spread over my skin. I did a quick check, and after confirming the people nearby were out of hearing range, I whispered back to my twin, "I will. Soon."

Turning around, I found several outdoor tables situated in front of the Italian diner. Two were filled with customers. *Great.* I looked both ways, because Grandma instilled that in me, and crossed the street. I opened the front door, and a bell rang out in the back.

A young girl carrying two plates of food approached me and smiled. Her bright red button sported the name "Kim." "Find a spot, and I'll be right with you."

"Thank you," I responded, then turned and grabbed an outdoor table away from the small group of diners.

While I waited, I stared at Trinkets. I tilted my head, but nothing changed. Bad. Blinked. Still bad. After taking out my planner, I flipped to the back section and jotted notes on what needed to be done. Power wash the brick. Check for mortar repairs. Clean the windows. Paint the door and redo the signage. I could do all of that, except the mortar repairs on the second floor. No way in hell was I going to climb that high. Roof? Was there roof access from inside? Three floors. There had to be an attic.

A flutter tickled my insides. An attic maybe holding real antiques? Antiques bursting with emotional energy so strong, I'd have a movie instead of flashes going through my mind. *Oh goody.*

"Welcome to Calabretti's. What can I start you off with to drink?" the petite young Kim asked.

"I'll take a cup of tea with honey and creamer, please."

"Sure," she responded and handed me a menu. "Take a look, and let me know what you'd like. I'll be right back." She whipped around and headed inside.

I waited until after I'd ordered and eaten before questioning the waitress. My stomach was sated, and since Steph hadn't made a reappearance, my mind was clear. I'd taken the time during breakfast to write additional notes on my plans for the next few days. Lists—my best friends.

When Kim brought me my bill, I gave her my credit card. "By the way, I've just inherited Trinkets across the street, and I'm new to the area."

Kim gave me a big grin. "I know. I loved going there when I was little. My mom used to make it a Sunday visit." She laughed then continued in a low voice, "I used to think it had hidden treasures if I could only find them. You are planning on reopening it, right?"

"Kim!" A gorgeous tall man with black, curly hair and sharp features popped his head out the door. "Kim, I need you inside a minute. We've got a..." He paused and stared at me.

My heart pounded, and my jaw dropped. Oh man. His t-shirt hugged his muscular shape like a second skin. Black jeans stretched snug on long, lean legs and stopped at black leather shoes. I clamped my lips shut and waited.

After scanning me from head to toe, he swept his gaze to Kim. "A group of twenty arriving in fifteen. Help me get some tables moved together."

I inhaled quickly and rose to leave when Kim touched my arm.

"I have to run your card first," she said.

Behind her, the man had disappeared inside. I checked.

Heat rushed across my face. "Oh right, sorry." I returned to my seat.

"It's okay. He has that effect on women." She spun away and left me there staring at her back.

I was wearing yesterday's clothes, and my hair had to be a mess. I sighed. His stare had to be because I looked like I'd recently dragged myself off the street. Maybe that was a good thing. No reason to try attracting anyone. But still, I could look. *And what a view.*

The time it took Kim to return gave me opportunity to regather my wits and remember what I was going to ask her. I signed the receipt and left with directions to the closest hardware and grocery stores.

****

A few hours later, I returned home, and as soon as I entered the back door, the kitten was nipping at my feet. I frowned. Where was she relieving herself? Cat urine was horrible to remove from fabric. I sniffed. No smell around here.

"Please be litter trained," I whispered.

A Timed Wager: Lost Trinket Series Book 1

After placing the new litter box in a secluded area and showing it to my new resident, I headed upstairs to give her some privacy. She followed, letting me know in very loud sounds how hungry she was. I guess she wanted to eat first.

"I know, I know. I got you real food now."

I placed a little bowl on the kitchen floor and poured a little milk in it. Then I set another bowl near her and dumped in a small can of food. She promptly left the milk and inhaled the food. Chuckling, I moved away and started emptying the grocery bags.

"You eat too fast, you'll get sick," I warned her.

Well, hell. I sounded like my grandmother. After putting everything away, I flipped over my grocery list and checked the cupboards for dishes and such. I couldn't eat at the diner forever, but from the barren caves of the cupboards, it might still be my best source of cooked food. Why hadn't I thought to check for pots and pans? Did Aunt Caroline ever cook? There were no pots, pans, or cookware to be found. She didn't even have a microwave here. At least I got paper plates at the store so I wouldn't have to wash. But that wasn't going to help cook. *Shoot.*

Sherrie Lea Morgan

Most antique stores carried cast iron pots and pans. I hoped this one did too. I headed down to check.

Chapter Five

I scowled at my dirt-streaked face in the bathroom mirror. The lights lit up every smear, making it look like I'd recently cleaned a chimney. After sweeping, dusting, mopping, and wiping every surface upstairs, I was beat. I snacked on the items I'd bought at the store, but with no microwave or pots, hot meals would not be on the menu tonight. Why Caroline didn't have any cast iron pots in her antique shop was one thing I refused to worry about.

I discovered the laundry room along with an office and one other bedroom. Laundry couldn't be done without soap, which didn't get on my list, and the office contained one desk, filing cabinet, and chair. No overhead light at all.

The sun was close to setting now, and the long shadows of evening appeared. I still needed to go through the desk and filing cabinet to make sense of the yellowed papers that poked out of the drawers like straw from a scarecrow.

Basics first. I had to eat if I wanted to do more today…or tonight, rather.

"Just grab a shower and go over there," Steph said from behind.

"No, I'm filthy and with what I have planned after dinner, I'm going to get even dirtier. No sense showering right now and getting another set of clothes dirty, only to repeat when I go to bed."

"So, call and see if they have take-out. Or, better yet, if they deliver."

The image of that man flicked in and out of my mind. Just as quickly, pictures of him without a shirt…pants…that mouth, those eyes. I squeezed my eyes shut and shuddered.

"Uh-oh, what's this?" Steph asked.

"Nothing. That's a great idea though." I rushed past her to find my phone in the other room. I went to the window and peered out across the street. Calabretti's Italian Diner in large red letters lit up the street and its rooftop. I found the phone number painted next to the front door. Punching the numbers in, I held my breath. What if he answered?

"What if who answered?"

"Steph! No mind-reading, you promised."

"Fine, fine. It was only a quick peek, so now I have to know who you're thinking about if I can't look inside."

"Someone who works across the street. A cook or manager or something. He's hot. I'm not chasing, just enjoying the thought, okay?"

"Oh, okay. Be right back."

She evaporated before I could stop her. *Dang it*. She was going to go over there to look around. Not a bad idea really, but not right either. *Whatever.*

"Calabretti's," a bright woman's voice answered.

Drat, my luck sucked. "Um, yes. I was wondering if you offer takeout or delivery?"

"Takeout, yes. Delivery, no. I'm sorry. But we do have a takeout window that you can walk or drive up to, whichever is more convenient for you."

"Okay. I'll do that. I'm just moving in and don't have a computer to pull up your menu. Do you have like a lasagna dinner available?"

"Absolutely," she responded and itemized the menu items for me.

After giving my order, I went to the bathroom to at least make myself presentable through a window. My hairbrush would need a washing, too, after this.

The kitten had followed me throughout most of the day. She napped, however, when it came time to mop. I appreciated that and her company. Steph's visits were hit and miss most days, although she did visit every day. I prepared food for my four-legged friend and grinned when she scarfed her dinner.

"I'm going to have to name you, you know. Especially if we're going to be family."

She ignored me and turned to start cleaning herself. *Cats.* I walked down the stairs and found a little embroidery framed panel on the wall. *Harmony* was embroidered in a deep red thread sprinkled with golden ones. Sure, that sounded good.

"Be back soon, Harmony," I said, trying it out.

The responding meows gave me my answer.

At the takeout window, I tapped the buzzer and waited. I dug out my card as the window slid open.

"I was wondering how long it would take before I'd get a chance to meet you."

His voice slid like warm honey in my veins. My gazed jumped up to meet his chocolate eyes with golden flecks that glittered against the soft tan of his skin. His grin revealed straight white teeth, and my mouth opened partly in anticipation of leaning forward and tasting his skin. My tongue tickled at the image of licking and nipping his chin. He shifted and I glanced back to his eyes which had darkened.

"Go on. I won't tell," he whispered, then gave me a secretive smile.

A shudder rippled through me, and I grabbed the metal shelf outside the small window, letting the edge cut into my palm. *No. No. No. I will not kiss a complete stranger.* I forced my lids closed and dipped my head. That way, when I opened them, I'd only see my purse. Wicked, wicked man.

Pulling out my card, I tried to laugh it off but coughed instead. I stared at the dark crisp curls that peeked above his stark white t-shirt. Oh my god. My fingers curled. *Stop it. Stop it right now.*

I handed over my card. *Pretend you didn't hear him. Pretend he's just another man. Do whatever it takes to get your food and get the hell home.*

I plastered a smile on my face. "Hello. I'm Shannon and I just moved in across the street. Your breakfast menu was great. Since my kitchen isn't quite stocked, I might be a regular customer here for some time. It's a nice place. I've never visited before."

He laughed a sweet, deep chest laugh that crinkled the skin near his eyes and enhanced the dimple in his chin. "Nice save, Shannon. I must be getting rusty on my flirting techniques. It's good to meet you. I'm Mitch, by the way. Let me get your food."

I dropped my shoulders when he turned away. *Great, interesting woman turned blithering idiot in less than five minutes.* At least he was honest. I could do this.

When he returned, I grinned. "You're not getting rusty." I winked and walked away with his chuckle following in my wake.

Chapter Six

I straightened and closed the top front drawer I'd been pawing through. Steph's laughter bounced against the walls of the small office. With a quick tour below, I had absconded with a fifties' desk lamp, a seventies' floor lamp that looked like an overgrown pod, and an old cloth-braided throw rug. Eclectic look, but the items held no flashes of images from previous owners when I touched them and lit up the office perfectly for an evening of discovery. A glass ashtray held the incense cone I'd lit earlier, giving the room a nice aroma of sage.

"I didn't think it was funny," I chided, biting my inner cheek to keep from joining her.

"Uh-huh. I wish I'd been able to see your face," Steph responded when she shifted to sit on the floor under the window.

Harmony entered the room and sashayed to weave around my ankles before curling into a small ball under the desk.

"Harmony, how are you doing?" Steph asked. "I think momma's got the hots for the Italian man across the street."

"Steph!"

"You do. I went on a hunt over at the diner while you were busy acting like a teenage girl with uncontrollable hormones."

"Bite me." Did I really want to know what she found out? Not that it mattered. She'd tell me anyway. I ran my hand over Harmony's back and scratched her neck. Her eyes were closed, and she purred stronger than a '65 Mustang. Such loudness for a little thing. I considered Steph sitting there appearing as I once did at the age of seventeen. Normally, she kept to my age. "How come Harmony doesn't react to you? Can she see you? And really? You're sticking with seventeen?"

"She does. She chooses not to acknowledge me," Steph said. "I can age when I want, and right now, I like this look." She flipped the ends of her short bob, the same style I used to wear.

"Why?"

"She doesn't need to. I'm no threat, and I'm not hers. You are."

"Casper interacted with you, and he never knew you before either."

"Casper belonged with Grandma Brenda. We were hers. Or something like that, I think." She rolled her shoulders. "Whatever. You want to hear what I found out?"

"Sure," I said and tugged on the bottom drawer to the desk. It snagged then squeaked, but didn't pull out.

"Mitch is the owner of Calabretti's. Apparently, he took over after his parents retired and moved to Florida."

I nodded, tugging harder on the drawer. I jiggled it and shoved it in, then pulled it out again, ignoring the sounds of wood rubbing and squeaking in protest against my assault. The drawer gave and opened. Inside sat a metal box.

"Oh, a metal box. Metal boxes always contain important things," Steph said as she scooted closer.

"Right. Is he single?" I asked while I lifted the box and set it on the desk.

"Yep, never married. Close once, but broke it off. You going to check for images?" She leaned her hip against the desk.

I jerked open the first drawer I'd investigated and grabbed the small silver key I'd seen there. "I did. Nothing." After plugging the key in the lock, I twisted. It clicked. "How'd you find out he broke it off just by eavesdropping?"

"Aren't you going to open that?" Steph asked, leaning over and pointing to the box.

I opened it. Inside sat a book and an old pocket watch. I glanced at Steph. "So, how did you find out?"

"Seriously, Shan? There's a book in that box that looks like a diary, and you're not opening it up?"

I lifted my hands and waved my fingers in her face. "I'm not touching anything that looks as old and personal as those two items without gloves. You know better."

"Ugh!" Steph spun around and started to fade.

"Wait!" I called out, but she'd gone.

How did she know Mitch had called his wedding off?

****

I stared at the contents of the box. Curiosity won. *It's old and likely holds older and faded memories. It should be safe.* I took several deep breaths. Then, very slowly, I lifted the pocket watch and held it between my palms. Closing my eyes, the images came onto the white board I envisioned. Two older men sat together smiling and laughing, and a gray-haired one held the watch. The other darker-haired man looked like an older version of the sleazy pawnshop owner Bobby. Another image of the gray-haired man appeared. He had the pocket watch in his hand and was checking the time. He frowned at the clock on the wall of something like a hospital hallway. It disappeared quickly and was replaced by another image of the same man sitting at a table at Calabretti's, staring across the street. A woman waved at him from the walk in front of Trinkets, and he waved back.

I dropped the watch back into the drawer and rubbed my palms together. Whoever the two men were, one had to be related to Bobby. There was no name on it. Why did Aunt Caroline have his watch? I surveyed the other items, and a money clip with the name *Green* on it glinted in the lamplight. I lifted it and immediately received an image of the dark-haired man again. He rubbed the clip and placed it in his pocket. The image shimmered then cleared to show the man signing a paper.

I closed the drawer, tucked the money clip in my pocket, picked up Harmony, and headed down the hall.

I'd figure it out tomorrow. Right now, I needed to shower and get to bed. My muscles were begging me to give them a rest already.

****

The morning sun lit up my bedroom like a summer day. Clean windows. Gotta love them. I stretched out the kinks and hopped up. Time to get the day going. I fed Harmony, ate a breakfast bar, and headed out. If I was lucky, I could have that front side washed before too many people crowded the street.

Bobby and Mitch seemed to be doing fine with the tourists and locals in town. The other businesses seemed to have a small but steady customer base as well. Hopefully, this would work for Trinkets too.

Four hours later, I stood on the sidewalk in front of Trinkets, soaked from head to toe and grinning like a kid at a candy shop. The power washer cleaned away all the layers of dirt and dust on the front masonry.

I peered toward the pawnshop. Bobby had tried to strike up a conversation earlier, but I'd been in full power wash mode to stop. The sun had dried most of the brick, and the dark red stones gleamed in the afternoon light.

With that and the now clean exterior side of the windows, Trinkets now appeared closed but not abandoned.

That should appease the town council...for now. I still needed to get the sign fixed and at least set up a window display. I frowned. Setting up the displays meant I'd have to figure out what to put in them.

A bell jingled next door as an older woman left the small quilt shop. I glanced at the time and grinned. I hadn't had a chance to meet the owner of *I Sew You Knot* quilt store. Since she was the only person separating me from Bobby's place, I ran over to introduce myself.

As I reached for the door handle, the door blinds dropped and a loud click sounded. A small frail hand slipped between the blinds and the window to flip the sign to *Closed*. I shifted to peek in the window and saw no movement. Weird. Where did the owner of that hand go? She wasn't hiding from me...was she?

Chapter Seven

After lunch, I finished sanding the last of the dingy white paint chips from the front door. The tall buildings on my side of the street blocked the glaring sun from burning my skin as I worked. The painter's tape took a bit of effort, but I finally got the decorative hinges, handle, and bolt lock covered. Not too shabby for a beginning. I stood a few feet away with sweat dripping down my back while light wind played with the various pieces of hair that had escaped my braid. The afternoon sun dried most of my power wash shower, but my clothes still clung to me like a second skin.

"Looking good, beautiful," Bobby announced when he joined me on the sidewalk.

I slid a glance at him and then back at my work, holding stock-still against the shudder that threatened to turn the day awkward. If only he'd quit trying to undress me with his eyes. Creep, but neighbor just the same. I'd be polite if it killed me.

"Thanks, Bobby," I responded. The picture of the money clip flashed in my mind. "Oh, I have something I think might belong to you." I left him standing there and rushed inside. I grabbed the money clip I'd left by the back door, returned to him, and held out my hand. The clip had his last name on it. The watch didn't. I had to be sure before I gave up the watch too.

"A gift? And we haven't even had dinner yet," he joked.

"I found this while cleaning upstairs." I handed him the clip I'd wrapped in tissue. "I found the name Green etched on it and thought it might belong to someone in your family."

Bobby unwrapped the item and gasped. With his fist wrapped around it, he waved it at me. "How did you get this?" he demanded. His face reddened.

I took a step back. "I told you, I found—"

"Liar! I knew Billy Ray had someone helping him. Your little act of innocence ain't going to work with me, lady!"

What? He moved close enough that I could see the blister forming on his upper lip. *Ouch.*

His body shook as he continued spitting words at me. "This was my grandfather's, you little bitch. I wondered where this went. You lied about recently moving in. Likely you stole the keys to this place after you and Billy Ray figured it'd be easier to live in town and steal than doing it from outside. Or have you decided to go on your own since your little spin with Billy Ray ended? I bet you've been working on a good story to be here permanently. You and Billy Ray failed years ago, and if you think you're gonna do any better on your own, you're fooling yourself."

Little bits of his spittle threatened to land on my face, and I shifted away. My stomach churned, and my throat locked up. What the heck was wrong with him? Who was Billy Ray?

"I'm calling the cops. They're going to arrest you and lock up your fine little ass…and Billy Ray's. I'm gonna sue you both for all the money I spent on lawyers."

"I'm not a thief. I really did—"

"Liar. Green's Pawn Shop is mine, and ain't no one taking it away. You're in for it now," he hissed while he pulled out his cell phone and began punching numbers.

What happened? A buzzing began in my ears, and I blinked several times. *Breathe. Breathe.* Where was Steph? She always showed up at times like this. The one ghost I knew had picked the wrong time to not make an appearance.

My heart pounded against my ribs when he relayed information over the phone. He told them my name and where we were. *Oh no. No. No.* If they demanded proof, I wouldn't be able to explain without showing them the diary or explaining my gift.

"What's going on?" Mitch's deep voice broke in to my rambling thoughts. My body shuddered again. "He's calling the police. He thinks I stole something that I found inside that belonged to his grandfather. He mentioned someone named Billy Ray?"

"Come on. I've been watching you all morning, and it's dinner time. You need to eat." He tugged on my elbow.

"Shouldn't I stay here? What if the police come?"

"You're only going to be across the street. Don't worry. It'll be okay. Bobby there will rant on his phone for at least another half an hour before he hangs up.

Besides, he'll be able to keep his eye on you. We'll sit outside."

I nodded and followed Mitch across the street. My stomach clenched with each step, and my chest pounded like a wild monkey decided to make it his personal set of drums. My legs shook, and my body moaned at me, preparing to blank out. *Not happening*. When we reached the outdoor patio, I dropped into the closest empty chair and slumped over the table.

"Let me get you something," Mitch said and headed inside.

I couldn't even enjoy his presence and the tingles his voice promised. Darkness, like a ton of dirt, began pouring over me.

"What on earth is wrong with you?" Steph's voice resounded in my head and I jerked. "You're acting like it's the end of the world. When did you turn into a drama queen?"

My blood stirred, and my lips clamped together. I shook my head and closed my eyes. *Sure, now she shows up.*

"Well, at least you're not getting arrested in front of a crowd," she said. "Don't pout. Your man is returning."

46

Pout? I wasn't pouting. I was panicking. She really needed to learn to read me better. Some twin she was. I straightened my back. When Mitch returned, I grinned.

"Thanks so much. All that work has worn me out," I said when he set a plate with a club sandwich in front of me. How on Earth did he expect me to eat?

He handed me a tall glass of tea. "Drink this first so I can refill it. You're probably a little dehydrated too."

I drank it all obediently and returned the glass. "Thank you."

"I said not to worry about Bobby. This isn't the first time he's acted this way. Eat or else."

"Or else?" I asked.

He grinned and winked, then walked away again.

I sighed. My insides fluttered then settled. *Better.*

I checked across the street, and sure enough, Bobby still talked on the phone, walking back and forth and waving his hands. I shook my head and turned to my sandwich. My stomach growled its pleasure, and I bit in. Warmth swept through me, and my muscles instantly eased. This was what I needed.

Mitch returned with two glasses and sat opposite me. He studied me while he lifted his glass. "What color are you going to paint it?"

I stared at him, my mind empty and my mouth full of soft ham and cheese. *Paint what?* I tilted my head. I never talked with my mouth full. Grandma taught me that.

"The front door," he indicated with his hand.

Oh, that. Right. I swallowed the last bite and studied the front of Trinkets, refusing to look at Bobby who still had the phone to his ear. "I haven't decided, actually. I don't want to go back with white." I leaned forward. "Are you sure it's okay to ignore him like this? Do you know who Billy Ray is?"

Mitch chuckled. "Absolutely sure. The more attention you give him, the worse he gets." He shrugged. "When Bobby's grandfather died a while back, his cousin Billy Ray claimed he had a right to the pawnshop. They went to court and Bobby won. Nothing more to add, really."

At that moment, the meter officer arrived and sidled up next to Mitch. She laid her hand on his shoulder and leaned in, brushing her chest against his arm while staring

48

at me. "So, you're the new owner of Trinkets. What brings you to our little town?"

Chapter Eight

Mitch frowned and stood, shrugging off her hand. She grabbed the back of the metal chair he'd vacated as if she was caught off balance, and it tilted with her weight. She scowled.

Whatever.

Mitch grabbed my empty plate and winked at me. "Give her time to settle in, Nancy. It's only been a few days," he said over his shoulder while he walked away.

She scanned me from head to toe, shrugged, and walked away without even saying 'bye.

Well, okay then. I finished my drink while Bobby stomped back to his pawnshop. I stood at the same time Mitch returned.

He pulled the chair back with his large hand. "Have dinner with me Friday night?"

My eyes widened, and my lips parted. Was he serious? His glance dipped slightly, and he stared at my mouth. Oh, wow.

"Um, what about your diner? Aren't Fridays the busiest night for you?"

"True, but it won't fall apart if I'm not here," he said.

"Oh." I continued to stare.

"Say yes," he whispered.

"Yes," I whispered back. Really, I whispered. How could I not while drowning in those eyes of his?

"Good. I'll pick you up at your back door at seven."

"I can walk over here," I suggested.

Mitch grinned. "Oh no. Not here. I'm not about to have our dinner watched like a movie by everyone in the neighborhood. We're going into Augusta where we can have a nice private dinner."

I nodded. Made sense to me. "Okay."

He pointed across the street at Bobby with his chin. "Don't worry about that. My cousin, Rick, is the local law enforcer. I'll have a talk with him for you.

"Thanks." I walked in a daze back into the shop, up the stairs, grabbed Harmony from her perch on the rocking chair in my room, and dropped on the bed.

I stared at the ceiling. Why did Bobby accuse me of stealing the money clip? Why did Aunt Caroline have it? I petted Harmony and tried to consider all the possibilities.

She scooted and began her patty cake thing against my side. Her claws squeezed and dug into my skin with little pinpricks. Not too painful and it was the way of cats, so I stayed still.

I could've read that diary psychically or normally. I frowned. Depending on how often she wrote in it, I'd be asking for years of images to flood in my head. No, it'd be too much. I should read it normally. A few images from one object, I could handle. Not a whole lifetime of them.

Harmony finished her thing, curled up, and snored in a little ball on my pillow. I rose and headed into the office, grabbing my gloves along the way.

The afternoon sun peeked through the sheer curtains I'd hung up yesterday. I sat and inhaled several breaths while I pulled on my gloves to read the diary. The air freshener filled the room with lavender and steadied my heart. I cleared my mind, just in case, and opened the drawer. Picking up the book, I opened it.

September 12, 1955 – Today was no harder than any other day. Beth is doing well, and the ladies at the deaf school have been so helpful getting me a job with them. I finally got out of that empty warehouse, and now I can really take care of my daughter. We eat three meals a day, and Beth is growing fast. She seems happier around the other children and picked up sign language very fast. I miss mom and Brenda so much. But I can't ever go back. It's not right that Dad thought I couldn't take care of Beth. If he could see me now... No, I can't say that. I don't think it would matter. He'd take her from me. I know better. I don't care why Mom stays with him anymore. She wouldn't have fought for me, so I won't fight for her. It's better this way. I'm safe and so is Beth. That's all that matters now.

Wow. So Caroline ran away? She couldn't have been more than seventeen when her daughter was born. In that time, a single woman with a child would definitely cause curiosity, unless she came up with a good background story.

I set the book down and went to the window, tugging off my gloves. People of various ages walked along Main Street, peeking in some windows, going in some shop doors. Maybe some would come in here. *Not yet. I'm not ready yet.*

Across the street, Mitch chatted with diners. I rolled my eyes. I'd accepted his invitation to dinner. What was I thinking? *Drat.*

I ran into my room and whipped open the closet door. Empty hangers hung all along the rack, barren of anything but one lone light green dress. Thank the heavens. I pulled it out and inspected it. It would work with a little jewelry added. I sighed. I had no nice jewelry. I could afford a couple pieces if I found some on sale.

Leaning over, I dropped a kiss on Harmony's sleeping head and grabbed my purse. I needed only one or two items to spruce up the outfit. I stopped. I needed a shower first.

When I returned, I parked and got out. Beside the back door of Trinkets stood a man in uniform. His patrol car—well, truck really—sat behind Bobby's place. *Great.* Now I had to deal with the cops.

I approached him with a pleasant smile plastered on my face. "Good evening, officer. Ricky, isn't it?"

He grinned and held out his hand to shake. "I've already taken Bobby's statement and talked to Mitch. I'm here mainly to introduce myself and get your statement as well. If you have a few minutes, this shouldn't take too long."

"Sure. Did you want to come inside?"

"Nope. Like I said, this won't take long. You told Bobby you found the money clip while cleaning in Trinkets, right?"

"Yes. Yes, I did."

"Good enough." He scanned the back road and leaned forward, lowering his voice. "Are you the Stephanie Pryce that worked with BPD a few years ago on that missing boy case?"

I froze. My mind blanked as my head nodded.

His hand clasped my elbow. "It's okay. I don't share that kind of information with anyone. The police aren't keen on admitting when they've asked for outside help like you provide."

I nodded again and found my voice. "I really don't want that to be public information."

"It won't. I promise. But I have to ask you if that's how you knew the clip belonged to Bobby."

"It has Green etched on it."

He grinned. "True, but that's a popular last name."

"Here in this small town?"

"Bobby grew up here. His uncles live on the south side of town, and he has cousins all in Augusta. One of those cousins tried to say Bobby shouldn't have inherited the pawnshop. That money clip would have saved Bobby a ton of lawyer fees at the time. That's why he got so upset when you pointed him out as the owner of the clip."

Oh, great. "How would it have saved him money?" I had to know.

"Bobby's grandfather proclaimed to his entire family that whomever had that money clip owned the pawnshop. Bobby swore his grandfather promised to give it to him before he died. Only problem was, it went missing."

"Bobby thought his cousin Billy Ray hired me to steal it."

"Bobby may come across a bit...crass. But he really is a good guy once you get to know him. He never really learned social etiquette when it came to the ladies, if you get my meaning."

"I do."

He scanned the roads again. "He's helped me a lot when we had a rash of burglaries run through town last year. He doesn't want folks to know he's helping because being a jerk helps him negotiate his prices. I'm not sure he's fooling everyone. But since you're a single woman and new in town, I thought I'd let you know."

"I appreciate that. I really do. But I'm not ready to reveal my ability to anyone yet."

"No, I understand. I'm just saying that when you are— *if* you are—Bobby can be trusted to keep your secret. That's a code his grandfather made him live by…and Bobby loved his grandfather."

"I'll keep that in mind. Um…may I ask how you came across that information from Birmingham?"

His face turned a deep shade of pink. "I ran a check on you as soon as you showed up here. It's my town, so I like to know who's moving in."

"I see. Well, that explains it. I'll try to come up with a more creative way to return items if I find anymore."

"Either that or tell the truth. I'd offer to help, but I never was a good liar."

I laughed, relieved. "Good to know."

"By the way, Kim's my sister. She's always going on about how she can read folks. She said you're a good person. I agree. If you ever need anything…" He handed me his business card. "You give me a call."

"I will and thank you again." When he walked away, I spun around to go inside.

Harmony's call floated down the stairs, soothing my nerves. I headed up. Memories of the missing boy case threatened to flood my head. *No. No more nightmares.* I pushed the images out of my mind.

Chapter Nine

Friday morning, I woke to a piercing pain in my head. I squeezed my eyes closed, scooted farther under the quilts, and massaged my temples. Within minutes, Harmony joined me. After lapping at my hair a few times, she curled around the top of my head. The vibrating hum of her purrs filtered through the pain. *Darkness. I need darkness.* The light acted like pin pricks against my lids.

Images flashed in and out of my mind. I focused on building a brick wall to block the images. They seeped through cracks faster than I slapped on mortar.

"Are you sure you can't pinpoint a specific area? There's got to be at least an acre of woods here," the Sheriff said.

"It's been over three days, lady. We're likely to find him dead rather than alive. You shouldn't have given his parents such hope," the deputy said before turning to his boss. "I told you we didn't need the help of any psycho babblers involved in this."

59

Sherrie Lea Morgan

My heart punched its anger against my chest, the beats in tandem to Harmony's vibrations. My throat tightened, and I gasped for breath. *Stop it. Stop it.*

"Shan." Steph's voice weaved through the pain. "Shan, it's done." Her face appeared in my mind and blocked the nightmare images. "Shan, focus on my voice. Feel Harmony's purring and breathe."

I did. The pain faded as my body began shaking. Sweat dripped across my cheeks. The quilt pulled away from my head, and the soft colors of my crystals, caught by the morning light, cleared my vision when I lifted my eyelids.

"Steph?" I asked, my voice trembling.

"I'm here. It's done. Breathe, Shan," she whispered, and a cool breeze wafted around me. Her favorite lavender hand cream aroma filled my nostrils, and my body relaxed.

"Steph," I whispered.

"It's okay. Close your eyes again and rest. I'll stay and make sure they don't return."

"I miss you so much," I choked out and obeyed her request. My mind blanked and I slept.

****

That night, I stood in front of the mirror pressing a hand to my stomach. *I'm going to vomit. Really.* I swallowed a few times, breathed in and out slowly, and rolled my shoulders.

"It's not like you haven't gone on a date before, Shan," Steph said from behind me.

"I know. I'm still nervous. He's…different. I don't know him at all. What was I thinking?"

"He's hot, nice, and single. Why not? Did I mention he's hot? Those chocolate eyes of his and that black hair with all those curls… Yum." Steph chuckled then sat on the bed. "Did I mention he's hot?"

"Yep, you did."

"And Italians are known for their sensuality and love-making skills."

"Steph, really?" I faced her with my hands on my hips. "I'm not having sex with him tonight."

"Oh, but soon, then?"

I flung up my hands and turned away. Slipping on the new heels increased my five foot four inches by another two. Not bad.

"I can do this," I mumbled.

"Heck yeah, you can. Have a great time," Steph hollered from the hallway while she floated away.

I jumped when the doorbell rang. It went on like a dozen bamboo chimes billowing in a storm. What on Earth? I ran downstairs as if I could stop the ringing. *Right*. I whipped open the door as the last chime rang out to see Mitch standing there bent over laughing.

I couldn't stop the grin crossing my face. "Like my doorbell, huh?"

"Oh yeah..." He gasped. "My dad used to tell me about it, and I never believed him. Now I know."

His breathy laughter sent bolts of electricity over my skin, followed by tickles of air dancing in my belly. My knees nearly buckled, and I clutched at the doorknob. His deep mossy scent wafted inside, wrapping and weaving around me. *Oh my stars.*

"Let me grab my purse, and we can go."

"Sure thing," he said and waited inside the door.

I ran up, grabbed my purse, and we headed out. Walking to the car, Bobby's television blared from his place and drowned out the sounds of light traffic.

"So, you don't care for your neighbors knowing your business?" I asked.

"What?"

"The reason we're going out of town for this date."

"Oh, it's not that I don't want my neighbors to know my business. With a town this small, it's a given they'll find out the generalities. I'm not airing out my business in public. What these people find out, how they find out, is a whole bowl of mess. I get sucked in because I live here," he said, unlocking his car.

"So, what is it exactly?"

"If they're going to have fodder to talk about, at least it should be as close to the truth as possible. That way, when the gossip mill gets finished with their information, it's less likely to be completely wrong." He sighed and walked around to get in his side, then paused. "I've been burned very bad by dramatic gossip. I know what it can do to people's lives, and I'm not a big fan of it."

"I see."

Did it cause the breakup of his engagement?

Chapter Ten

Half an hour later, we entered the edge of what I assumed was Augusta, along with the sunset. The music floating in the car relaxed my nerves...a little.

"This is one of the historical districts. The homes here are fantastic. I prefer the brick facings of Petrie's, but I can't deny these beauties their due," Mitch said.

I slid a glance his way and then out my window. If I stared too long at his face, I'd turn into a blithering idiot. Houses sat side by side. White clapboards separated stone homes, and some had a small stretch of lawn between them. Most were in good condition, but some appeared sad and empty. Some had been turned into business offices which sat void of care, too. An image of Trinkets came to mind when I first saw the businesses. Trinkets wouldn't be mourning too much longer.

"I agree. I think I prefer Petrie's, even though I'm new to town."

"Not new anymore. You've been here for almost a week now. A few more and we'll consider formal adoption," he teased.

"I'm honored, I guess." What else could I say?

"You should be. Petrie's Crossing has history and roots going back to the height of the railroads," he said. "Have you been to Rocker's Rail Museum? It's at the end of Main Street."

I shook my head. "I saw the signs for it, but I've been working on Trinkets." *Trying to make it a home.*

"I know and you're doing a great job there. Listen"—he reached over and tapped my leg with his fingers—"I know someone who can redo that sign of yours."

Sign? What sign? His touch shot heat up my thighs. I clenched my jaw and focused on keeping still. I glanced at his large, tanned hand gripping the gear shift. It contrasted sharply against my light green dress. If I shifted... Oh lord, no. *No.* Hot images flashed through my mind, stronger than any psychic image ever had before. I inhaled sharply when the images refused to stop, and heat pooled low in my belly. Desire exploded.

In the secluded interior of his car, my gasp echoed, and I bit my lip, refusing to acknowledge it. Out of the corner of my eye, his jaw clenched, and his hand tightened so much, his knuckles turned white. His harsh breathing reached my ears. Images of him above me, touching me, kissing me filled my brain. I moaned. *Dear lord, what was happening?*

His grunt snagged my attention, and I turned his way. The car had stopped on the side of the road, and he turned to me with low-lidded eyes. His free hand grasped my shoulder to pull me to him.

I let him pull me close. I let him sweep down and take my mouth in a searing kiss. His lips erased the images dancing in my mind. His tongue licked around mine. I grasped the curls behind his ears and held on while he assaulted my lips. *More.* My body took over, and my mind blanked.

His taste, his smell, his touch quickened my pulse. He pulled away slightly, and cool air filled my lungs. His lips moved against mine once again.

"Woman, you are too tempting. I won't lie. I want more. But not here, not now," he whispered and pressed his forehead against mine.

I nodded once, taking in quick, deep breaths. Too much too soon. But dang, he tasted good. I closed my eyes and slowed my breathing. I shook myself mentally. *Stop it.*

I pulled away and gifted him with a smile. "You're right."

He kissed my temple and sat straight. He looked in the rearview mirror and pulled out into the road. His hand shook before he clamped it to the steering wheel. Within minutes, we arrived at the restaurant.

Thank goodness.

The evening wind cooled my body. My breaths steadied, and my need abated. I waited while Mitch spoke with the hostess. She offered a pleasant smile and asked that we follow her.

Mitch walked beside me but didn't touch me. After we were seated and gave our drink orders, the hostess walked away.

Mitch leaned forward. "You okay now?"

I nodded while heat infused my neck and cheeks.

"Please don't be embarrassed. I think we should continue what we were doing in a more private area," he said.

"We haven't known each other very long. I mean…I don't even know what your position is at the diner or much about you. I'm not normally like that." Lame, but a good enough excuse for now.

He chuckled. "Neither am I. I'd like to think I'm more of a gentleman. I'm not sure what happened." He shrugged. "However, to answer your questions. I'm thirty-two and have owned the diner on my own for the last three years since my dad died. I was born here in Augusta, but lived in Petrie Crossing all my life. I grew up getting coins flattened on the tracks and loved every minute of it. I'm single, too, in case you were worried."

"Oh, I knew you were single. I'm sorry to hear about your dad. I lost my parents when I was eleven, but it still hurts. Is the diner part of your family heritage, then?"

"Yes, it is. My ancestors came over from Italy and migrated down here along with the railroad. One of them was a big time investor in alternative transportation. I haven't done much research on it. I'm simply relaying the family stories I get during the holidays." He placed his hand over mine. "I'm sorry you lost your parents. That had to be rough at that age."

Our waitress arrived and poured us each a small glass of wine. She set two glasses of water on the table and took our orders.

I waited until she left before continuing. "My grandmother raised me, and it was fine. She was the younger sister of Caroline. You're an only child? I thought Italians preferred large families."

The light twinkled in his eyes before he threw back his head and laughed. He turned the heads of nearly every woman in the place, he was so handsome. "We do and I'm not an only child. I'm the only one living locally. I have six siblings scattered throughout this side of Georgia." He grinned. "Ms. Caroline had a sister? My mom never mentioned that."

"Oh," I responded.

What was it like with so many others? Heck, what was it like growing up with parents?

Chapter Eleven

After dinner, Mitch drove me home, keeping both his hands on the steering wheel. I'd had a great time and learned a lot about Petrie's Crossing during our talk. When we drew closer to home, my pulse picked up. Goodnight kiss time.

Mitch walked me to my back door with his hand on my elbow. When we reached the doorway, he spun me around, pushed me against the door, and pressed his body tight against mine. My mind blanked when he bent his head and devoured my mouth. I rushed to catch up and stroked his tongue with mine. He growled, grabbed my leg to wrap it around his hip, and rocked against my center, sending jolts of lust jabbing at my nerves. Instant wetness soaked my panties while his other hand cupped my breast.

My nipples hardened and I panted, running my hands up his chest and into his hair. I grabbed on to his head and hiked my other leg around his waist. His grunt

70

of approval blew past one of my ears as his mouth shifted to suckle and nip at my neck. I tilted to the side and gave him more access while my hips jackknifed against his, seeking release.

A door slammed. Mitch shoved my legs down, wrapped his arms around me, tucked my head into his chest, and hid me between the wall and his body. My body shook at the loss of heat, and I opened my mouth to ask what the heck was going on when he leaned in close.

"Bobby just came out. Likely to get a free peep show," he whispered, reaching behind me and opening my door a crack. He kissed my cheek, placed his hands on my shoulders, and gently guided me inside.

I turned in time to see him shut the door and hop in his car. I flipped off the exterior light and headed upstairs on the weakest knees I'd ever had.

****

An hour later, I sat in the office with Aunt Caroline's diary opened and wearing my gloves. I'd read to the eighth year she'd been living in Petrie's Crossing. The people she mentioned were grandparents of Mitch, Nancy, Officer Rick, and Bobby. Bobby's grandfather

71

Tim was a hoot. Did Bobby know his grandfather liked to sneak over here at night during the week when Beth went off to school and play poker? Not just any game of poker—strip poker. Naughty.

It was even more taboo in that day and age. Aunt Caroline literally beat the socks and clothes off that man every time. Ha. He'd let her win, I was sure. At least she was smart enough to realize that. I grinned and kept reading.

I've decided Tim needs to lose more than his clothes. I've started keeping a special box for my winnings. I know I'll have to return them one day. But, for now, I can look upon them during the time that Beth is home. She is growing up so fast, and the deaf school has taught her so much. I'm so very proud of her. I miss her. I've learned some sign language and we talk. But I'm afraid I'm losing her as each year she becomes more and more independent.

I sat back, staring at the walls. How hard must that have been to leave your family to provide for your child, only to have that child start pulling away from you? I grabbed the diary, flipped to the last few pages, and continued reading.

I don't think I have much time left. The doctors said only a year, and I'm going on my second one. I need to last long enough for

A Timed Wager: Lost Trinket Series Book 1

Lisa to turn eighteen. She's been sneaking off with that Grayson boy again. I tried talking to her, but I'm old now. She won't listen to me, and I can't get Beth involved. Lisa told me tonight she doesn't want Trinkets. I love this place and hate the idea of it sitting here empty. Or worse, being turned over to some stranger.

This town has been my saving grace. I wanted so much to give back to it. I tried telling Tim last week about what was happening to me. I couldn't. One day, he'll find out. I hope he doesn't hate me. He's asked me three times to marry him in the last ten years. It wouldn't be fair. He lost his first wife to this wretched disease. I won't make him go through that again. There has to be someone I can entrust Trinkets with. I am too tired too early these days. Two more years is all I ask for.

I miss you, Mom. I'm so sorry I left you and Brenda. I truly hope Brenda is happy. Brenda. I'll leave Trinkets to her and hope she doesn't burn it down in anger.

Obviously Grandma Brenda didn't burn anything. She didn't take care of it either. Someone did, though, or it'd be in worse shape.

But who the heck was Lisa? I grunted. That was what I got for skipping ahead. I dropped the diary back in the drawer, and an odd clunk came from the inside. *Weird.* I lifted the book out and inspected its spot in the drawer. It was bigger on the outside. I ran my fingers along the interior edges, and in the back, my thumb ran across a rough piece of cloth.

I grabbed my phone, turned the brightness up, and shined the light toward the back of the drawer. *There.* On the left, a small piece of leather loop stuck out of the corner. I reached in and very carefully tugged on the fabric. Squeaks pierced the room, and Harmony jumped off my lap and ran away. Scaredy-cat. I smirked and pulled more. The bottom of the drawer lifted away. As I slid it out, a long velvet bag bulging with something lay in the bottom. I poked it but nothing moved.

Like really, a snake or something could've been in there, right? I rolled my eyes and lifted the bag. After loosening the ties, I emptied the contents on the desk.

Rings, both fancy and worn, spun on the cherry wood top, dancing around a necklace, two watches, an earring hoop, and old photos. I pushed the photos around with my gloved fingers and peered close. A young woman and man stood smiling at the camera. The vignette photo enhanced the woman's light skin and the tanned shade of her partner.

Wait a minute. I leaned closer. That man looked familiar, like he could be Bobby's father. No, wait. That had to be his grandfather Tim. So, was the woman Aunt Caroline or Tim's wife? Why would Aunt Caroline have a picture of a man and his wife? No, that had to be Caroline.

"Looks a bit like Grandma Burns to me," Steph said in the shadows.

I regarded her white shadow then returned my attention to the photo. "You're right. She must be Aunt Caroline. From what she wrote in her diary, these things must belong to Tim, Bobby's grandfather." I frowned. "How could I return these without him accusing me of stealing again?"

The only way to do that would be to reveal my ability. *Not happening.* My shoulders dropped. *Small town like this? They'd never believe me.*

"Don't tell him. In this small of a town, the gossip would spread like wildfire. Sell them in the shop," Steph suggested.

"And have other people come in and find their grandparents' belongings on sale? Seriously?"

"Then hide them away and don't return them."

"I have to try, Steph. It's not right for me to have these items, and they belong to their rightful owners. Bobby, the creep that he is, still deserves to have his grandfather's belongings."

"Tell him you found it with the diary, and you read in there that it was his grandfather's."

"Then he'd demand to see the diary, and I'm not sharing something that personal with anyone. I can't do that. It's not mine to share."

"At least I warned you," Steph said before fading away into the darkness.

I stared at the cache of jewelry and sighed. Under one photo lay a smaller ring. Too small for a woman. I lifted it and checked for any engravings. Etched in cursive on the inside was the name Jack Mitchell Calabretti. Could that be a relative of Mitch's?

Chapter Twelve

L ate Sunday morning, I straightened my back and knocked on Bobby's rear door, ignoring the churning in my stomach and the pain prodding at my temples. This had to be done. Rick said I could trust him. He better be right. Besides, Mitch told me Bobby's cousin sat on the town council. Couldn't hurt to get some supporters there since it might be a while before I could actually open Trinkets for business.

The door swung open to reveal Bobby in a suit with the tie loosened and hanging free to bounce against his stomach, which threatened to break through every button that held on for dear life to its corresponding button hole.

It was Sunday morning. He'd been to church. *Okay, that could work in my favor, right?*

"Good morning, Bobby," I said with a small smile. "Do you have a few minutes? I'd like to talk to you about something."

"Listen, lady. I didn't push the issue with the cops because Gramps died a long time ago. I was too upset to realize you're too young to have been involved. Besides, Rick told me you didn't even live in this state until now. But that don't mean I think everything's on the up and up with you, you know."

"I know and I understand. If I were in your shoes, I'd feel the same." Not really, but I had to get on his good side.

"Hrmph," he snorted and opened the door wider. "I'm about to have some morning tea. You can have some if you want."

Bobby drank tea? Go figure. I followed him into the small break room he'd built off the back of his shop. Monitors hung on the back wall and displayed every corner of the shop on the other side of the closed door. *Smart*. He poured tea and I sat, taking small sips while he settled across from me.

"I know we might not have gotten off on the right foot," I said. "I want you to know that I inherited Trinkets from my grandmother who was the owner's sister. Caroline is…*was* my great aunt. It wasn't until

Grandma Brenda died that I even knew this place existed."

"Okay, makes sense. Still doesn't explain how you ended up with my grandfather's money clip." He leaned forward, frowning. "Or how Caroline ended up with it."

"Well, see, this is the thing. I have been going through every nook and crevice in the place, cleaning upstairs and all." When he didn't say anything, I continued. "That's how I found it. I don't know why Caroline had it or how she got it." I sat back and raised my hands then, let them drop. "You're the only Green I've met so far, which is why I thought it belonged to you. But I also found Aunt Caroline's diary. It appears that while she lived here—toward the end of her time here, I mean—she...well...she had a relationship with your grandfather."

He jumped up. "No, that's a lie. My gramps loved my grams until the day she died and after." He stomped over to the counter and back. "I watched him grieve until the day *he* died."

"Bobby," I pleaded. "Listen, please, they had a secret relationship. It was after your grandmother died. They used to play...poker. She won...a lot."

The man froze in mid-step and stared at me. He walked over and dropped in the chair across the table. "Gramps was awful at card games. Listen, lady. I want to believe you. I do. Being the neighborly thing and all." He heaved a deep sigh.

"Thank you. I appreciate it." I stood up. "I'd rather no one knows about the diary. I've only started reading the entries, and they're very personal. With the information I told you, others might try to demand to know if their relatives are mentioned in it. I don't want to cause trouble."

"I guess I could trust you to be telling the truth. Rick said you were good people." He nodded. "Okay, I'll keep your secret for now."

If he only knew the real secret I kept, he might not agree. I stopped, pulled the pocket watch out of my pocket, and laid it on the table. I leaned over and whispered, "I found this, too, with the money clip." Turning, I moved toward his back door.

"Wait." He pushed the watch toward me. "That's not mine." He coughed. "I mean, that didn't belong to my grandfather."

"You're sure?" Of course he's sure. Then who owned the watch?

He nodded.

I picked up the watch, tucked it away, and turned to leave. "Thanks," I said and left.

My steps were slow returning home. I walked in and through the back area of Trinkets and stopped in the middle of the store. I scanned the shelves and counters, which displayed everything from old signs to clothing and furniture. The stock wasn't huge, but not small either. I shuddered. So many possible memories stored in here. My gloves would definitely be used once I got started cleaning, which needed to be sooner rather than later. My savings account wouldn't last forever.

My shoulders dropped. Once I started cleaning, I'd be able to figure out a date to re-open Trinkets. Once it re-opened, then that would be that. No turning back. Only thing was…did I want this?

So many questions, like what was Aunt Caroline doing with one of Mitch's family rings? Who owned the pocket watch? Where was Beth now? Why didn't she or this Lisa girl want Trinkets? Who *was* Lisa?

And how long could I go without jumping Mitch's bones?

Chapter Thirteen

L ater that afternoon, I ate lunch at Calabretti's. Mitch had winked at me when I arrived, and it started my afternoon with a sweet buzz through my body. I ate my sandwich, letting the questions from earlier meander around in my head, trying not to freak out at the lack of answers. The afternoon breeze blew my hair about my face and cooled the air.

"Hey, lady," Bobby said with a big grin as he grabbed the chair across from me.

"Hey, Bobby, you doing okay?" I asked.

"Lots better now. Listen..." He pulled out a paper from his shirt pocket. "I made a list of some things I know my gramps used to have, and I'd really like to find them. Think you could look around and see if he lost them in a game?"

His face reddened as I stared at him, my mind blank. Then understanding hit me. *Ah, right.*

I flashed him a smile. "Sure. I'll look around," I promised, taking his list. I'd already paid, so I rose, and he followed suit. "Give me a day or two to search, and I'll bring you what I find."

"Thanks, I appreciate it," he responded. Suddenly, he grabbed me in a big, tight hug. Before I could react, he planted a wet kiss on my cheek. "You're a good lady."

"Well, I see our new neighbor is making good friends fast."

I jumped out of the embrace and turned toward the voice. Nancy, Mitch's clingy ex. *Great*.

"Oh, hey, Mitch," she said over my shoulder. "Did you know your new neighbor's got a beau already? You must have lost your touch, eh babe?"

I frowned while Bobby puffed out his chest like a peacock. *Drat that man*. I checked and caught the frown on Mitch's face. Surely he didn't believe her. No, it was something else. Shoot, it was probably our public display.

Mitch didn't look my way. "She's got a right to date whoever she wants, Nan. Leave her alone."

I sputtered and tried to explain, but Mitch had spun around and reentered the diner. I faced Nancy. The grin on her face spoke volumes. My blood boiled.

"Have a nice day, you two." She laughed as she sauntered away.

Steph whispered in my ear, "Should have planted her one in the face."

Bobby rushed away whistling. Of course he would. I stood there for I didn't know how long. My stomach clenched, and my chest ached as if I'd suddenly been punched. My hands started to shake. Oh, hell no.

I stomped across the street to Trinkets, yanked open the door, and found the step ladder. After placing it, I climbed up and took down the sign. Its wooden face rejected the layer of paint, and it dropped flecks over my arms as I carried it inside and set it on the back bench. Stomping back to the ladder, I folded it and brought it in, slamming the front door.

Digging through the back cabinets, I found Aunt Caroline kept a nice stock of cleaning supplies. The kind used to make the antiques shine. Sand paper, pliers, and rust remover.

Watch this, Petrie's Crossing residents. I'd show them what the new neighbor in town was capable of. I worked on the sign for an hour, and after a quick trip into Augusta for additional supplies, I went back at it.

Using a foil press technique, the name Trinkets shined in gold lettering against the background of a lightly stained wood. The brass chain links glistened under the fluorescent lights. The sun would rock this sign. I put it aside and ran upstairs to throw on the coveralls I'd purchased at the secondhand store near the edge of town.

Gloves on, hair tied back, face mask set. I cranked on the radio, covered the front windows with paper to block anyone from peeking in, and started cleaning. I only stopped to eat, drink, and feed Harmony. By eleven, I was exhausted. I dropped on top of the covers and slept.

The phone ringing jerked me out of sleep, and I reached over to peer at the caller ID. Unknown caller, it read. Not answering. Jumping up, I showered quickly, redressed, and hit the shop again.

"Don't you think you're pushing yourself a bit hard here just to prove a point?" Steph asked.

"Nope. I've made a decision, and now I'm keeping to it," I called over my shoulder. "I'm doing this."

"Good," she said and blitzed out.

Good. Right. Yes. I blanked my mind and kept cleaning.

****

S hortly before dinner on the third day of cleaning, I stopped to take stock of my progress. Hands on hips, I walked around the shop checking for any missed spots. Not perfect, but pretty darn close. The new bulbs in the overhanging lights lit the place nicely.

Food first and then I'd tackle the accounting books. Mr. Lawrence said nothing about money, so I'd likely have to front the opening costs. At least there wasn't rent to be paid. The utilities wouldn't be too high with the new lighting I'd installed. *Thank you, internet instruction videos.*

I grabbed a shower and dressed. I peeked through the curtains, and Calabretti's had every table filled. *Fine.* I searched the internet for a local delivery place, and Calabretti's was the closest. *Not tonight.* I was too tired to deal with anyone. I went into the kitchen and made a sandwich, gave Harmony dinner, and sat on the floor to eat.

"Are you going to avoid him forever?" Steph asked.

"No," I responded between bites of ham and cheese. "Besides, he's the one acting like a jerk. Not me."

"The shop looks great. I'm proud of you."

I grinned. "Thanks." Then I frowned. "I wish you were really here."

"If I were really here, *you* wouldn't be here."

"True." I told her about the ring and other items I found in the hidden compartment along with Bobby's confirmation of the pocket watch. "Why do you suppose she had that ring?"

Steph's shadow rippled. "I don't know. Does it matter?"

I shrugged. "I don't know. Maybe, maybe not."

"You need to figure out that pocket watch. As for the ring, why don't you do your thing with it and see?"

"I'm too close to Mitch now. If there's anything on that ring, I might end up with more than a couple visions. I'm not ready for that again."

"Shan, you gave the missing boy's parents closure," Steph said.

"The cost was too much for me."

Steph sighed. "What if Caroline won the ring off Mitch's grandfather...which I'm having a hard time thinking she'd be like that. Or maybe off of Bobby's gramps. That I'd believe."

I glanced her way, and my eyes widened. "I hadn't thought of that. If he was as bad as Bobby, he'd use someone else's jewelry to play a game or two with Aunt Caroline, right?"

"That's more believable than Aunt Caroline being a town thief. Do your thing with it to be sure?" She paused, fading in and out. "Either way, you have to return all those items...including that ring."

"I know that." It didn't make it easier to do since I couldn't deal with too many probing questions, especially if people found out about my ability.

"Yeah, I figured you did. I just feel obligated to say it once in a while."

"Where you going these days when you're not with me?" I asked.

"There's a lot of old homes around here. I'm checking them out to see if there might be someone like me around."

"Why? You lonely?"

"No, silly. I'm just being nosy." She laughed before fading out. "Besides, you never know what's out there." Her last sentence echoed in the darkness.

She had a point.

Chapter Fourteen

I flipped through the pages of Aunt Caroline's books while sitting at the sales counter of Trinkets. My laptop sat open among the various folders and papers I'd pulled out from the filing cabinet underneath. She kept accurate records of her sales. Thankfully. I searched and uploaded an inexpensive accounting program and plugged in the necessary information to monitor expenses. The numbers told me how much I'd have to sell to make utility payments.

Anything above that I could use to buy more merchandise or hire an accountant to help me figure out taxes. Either way, I needed to get the place open and try to make a profit within the next four months. By then, my savings account would be empty.

I could've used my laptop to run sales, but it'd be better to have a tower. I had to keep business separate from personal. New computer first, then set up website and link pages to help with the opening. And marketing.

Shoot. I knew nothing about marketing. I guess a few ads online along with the local papers would work.

Maybe I should go talk to other businesses in the neighborhood. If I help them, maybe they can help me.

Who did Mitch say ran that museum? The pamphlet I'd grabbed at the store yesterday said the local railroad museum opened every day at ten in the morning. I shrugged. It was time to get to know the neighborhood anyway. Today, I'd buy a computer and play tourist.

My phone rang, and the noise didn't echo as loud as before. Must've been the new items I'd placed up front. Before I could answer, it stopped ringing. No caller ID again. Grabbing my purse, I headed out to hunt for a cheap but good computer.

When I returned a couple hours later, Bobby stood outside my back door. I got out, grabbed my bags, and figured I'd drag in the computer after seeing what he wanted.

"Need help bringing anything in?"

"I don't know. If it's going to convince everyone you're my new boyfriend, I think I'll pass."

Bobby at least had the decency to flush. "Hey, lady, I'm sorry about that. That Nancy just can't give up on Mitch, and I couldn't resist causing friction."

"Huh. Since you apologized, can you grab that box in the back for me?" I asked and unlocked the door to hold it open for him. The box wasn't heavy, but it made him huff a bit. He needed to really get in better shape. "You were waiting for me?"

Bobby nodded and carried the box in. After setting it on the floor, he bent over to catch his breath. "Damn, lady, what'd you buy?"

"Just a computer tower."

"Must be one heck of a computer to be that heavy. Listen." Bobby shifted his feet. He wanted something else, of course.

Since he refused to look me in the eye, I spoke up. "Is there anything else?"

"Well…I was wondering if you'd had the chance to look for any more of Gramp's things?"

"Not yet. I've been working here, trying to get the shop ready to open." I waved my hand toward the front. "As you can see, it's been a long job in itself."

Bobby whistled as he walked into the shop. "Nice job. You have been working at this. I think the layout is better than the way it used to be." He returned to me with a smile. "Okay, I won't bother you again about it." The worry lines around his eyes and forehead sharpened.

"I'll do a pass this weekend," I promised. "That's two days from now. If I find anything, you'll know right away."

"I can handle that. Thanks. I'll be getting out of your way, then."

He left and I shrugged. Digging into the box, I set up the computer and register space for sales. The receipt machine took less space than an old time calculator. Progress definitely had its perks. I glanced at the clock. Tourist time would have to wait.

Outside, I studied the freshly stained front door of Trinkets. A few steps back and I reviewed the overall scene. It was nice. Attractive without being flashy and it stood out. The light lavender color popped against the red brick. Once I figured out what hours the store would keep, I could hang the sign and open the doors. But at least the exterior looked good, and the town council wouldn't have a chance to fine me.

My stomach growled, and Harmony's cries carried down the stairs. I put away my tools and got her fed. After showering again, I put on clean clothes and headed out to eat. Time to see the gorgeous Italian man who made my insides melt like butter, whether he was ready to see me again or not.

Chapter Fifteen

I fell into bed and groaned. Mitch hadn't made an appearance the entire time I ate. A sudden rush of customers from a tourist bus unloaded, and Kim politely urged me to wrap up my meal to make room for the newcomers.

Harmony sidled up and did her patty cake thing against my shoulder, then wrapped around my head like a turban. Her snoring vibrated against my forehead. I'd try again tomorrow to see him. Pfft. Like a lovesick puppy. Was I lovesick? *No. Not that.* I closed my eyes and forced my mind blank.

The next morning, after snacking on a breakfast bar, I got to work clearing space in the store and moving items I would not sell into a back closet. I'd ask around later to get those donated somewhere. My arms ached from lifting, and my stomach growled. I glanced at the time. *Lunch. Food. Mitch.*

Someone knocked on the front door.

I sighed and rubbed my stomach. "Soon," I promised my now rumbling stomach. I opened it to a tall woman with short cropped ebony hair and a small crooked nose. I smiled and opened my mouth to greet her, but she pushed the door open farther.

"My name is Judy Elrod, curator of Rocker's Museum." She stepped past me and wrinkled her nose. "I'd heard the new owner was settling in. I wanted to speak with you before you open for business." She stormed left to stand before the side bay window. The light pierced through to spotlight the corner display of railroad memorabilia I'd found and set up. She waved at the exhibition. "Those items belong in my museum, not an antique store."

My mouth dropped open, then I coughed. "Hello, I'm Shannon." Two could play this game. I moved to block her from going farther. "I've only recently arrived and have not taken stock of the merchandise here yet. Once I do, I will be happy to donate any verified relics to your museum. I don't approve of keeping historical items from museums." I used Grandma Burns's condescending tone to the best of my ability. It seemed to work.

A Timed Wager: Lost Trinket Series Book 1

Judy sniffed and headed for the door, her short heels clicking with each step. "I do hope you have reputable individuals who can verify the difference."

I stared at her retreating back. Reputable individuals? Who talked like that? What was her problem? First the quilt lady at the shop next door shunned me, then this lady snubbed me. What a weird town I'd moved to. I followed out the door and, after locking up, spun around and crossed the street.

Attempt number two. I headed for Calabretti's. Grabbing an empty seat, I waited for the server to arrive. I paced my breathing and ignored the chatter around me. Kim arrived with a glass of water and took my order. As soon as she left, I downed the liquid. The ice cold pierced the burning in my stomach and it cramped. *Great.* I sat with my back to the diner and stared down the street. Judy kept up a brisk pace away from Trinkets until she reached and entered Rocker's Museum.

"Here you go. Enjoy," Mitch said and set my dinner plate on the table. The normally loud lunch chatter volume dropped to a murmur. *Terrific. Everyone wants a show. I am not stooping that low.* I faced forward and refused to acknowledge anyone.

"Thank you," I said before stuffing the pizza slice in my mouth. The crust tasted like a paper plate dusted with dirt, and it sat in my dry mouth. I chewed and tasted nothing, keeping my eyes focused on the plate. I really wanted to speak to him, but not with an audience.

Mitch stood next to me. Out of the corner of my eye, his black jeans remained still like a tree in the dead of winter. A few inches separated my shoulder from his thigh. My body leaned and I jerked. Would he move? Should I say something? I looked up and smiled. Would *he* say something? After an agonizing moment that seemed like hours, he nodded and walked away. I held my breath, and suddenly the chatter of the diners grew in volume.

The air whooshed out of my lungs, and I dropped the slice onto the plate. What a waste. I sat there while it cooled. Kim returned fifteen minutes later, and my food still sat on the plate.

"Did you want a to-go container for that?" she asked.

I shook my head and kept my eyes averted. "No, thanks." I pulled out a ten which would give her a generous tip and allow me to leave immediately. Handing it to her, I rose and headed home.

I will not look back. I will not give anyone the satisfaction of seeing anything wrong. I will not give up.

I slowly undressed in the darkened corner of my room. Harmony mewed from her corner of the bed. I crawled in and petted her while the tears built. *Dang it.* The tears fell, and I rolled onto my stomach to silence the sobs that escaped. I didn't want Stephanie to hear me and come running to try to make things better.

Heaviness pressed on my back and legs. My muscles weakened, and my chest hurt from crying. I sniffled in the wetness of my pillow. Maybe living in this fishbowl was a bad idea. Maybe trying to start over was a bad idea. Or maybe I needed to stop acting like a crybaby, pull up my big girl panties, chalk the day up as a bad one, and get on with it. *Ugh.*

Chapter Sixteen

Pinks and purples danced through my lids as the morning sun peeked in and flashed its rays through the crystals I'd hung around my bedroom. I opened my eyes wide and grinned at the array of colors splashed on my walls. Like a beautiful watercolor, the light spread across the room and blurred bright colors into the corners and on my comforter. I inhaled deep and stayed there, staring at the scene.

After a bit, I glanced at the time. The diner would open in two hours. Hopefully I could come up with some way to get Mitch alone to talk. Why hadn't he reached out to me?

This store was home now, along with Harmony and the town. I didn't want to give up. Harmony climbed onto my chest and proceeded to clean my chin. Her course tongue scraped, and I shifted to the right. She grunted and scampered around to start the process on my hair. At least there it wouldn't take off a layer of skin.

A Timed Wager: Lost Trinket Series Book 1

I let her do her thing for a moment before rising and heading into the shower. The scene from yesterday flashed through my mind. Mitch hadn't outright ignored me. Maybe he was waiting for me to do or say something. It wasn't like we were smart enough to exchange phone numbers. We lived across the street from each other, for goodness sake.

I stepped out after washing and dried off, then tossed on a nice top and shorts. Tying my shoes took a bit longer because Harmony considered the laces her own special toys.

"I guess I have to get you some toys now," I told her.

I stood and brushed out my hair. After setting it in a long braid, I threw on minimal makeup. My war paint.

I am not giving up this shop. I'm not giving up a possible relationship with a very handsome man. I'm staying here, dang it. By the end of the day, the neighborhood will know that Shannon Pryce is no quitter.

In my office, I put on my gloves and opened the bag from Aunt Caroline's hidden compartment. After setting aside the little ring belonging to Mitch's family, I separated all the other items, giving them a good two-inch gap from each other.

I took off my gloves, then grabbed my notebook and pen and began to read each item, noting the images, descriptions, and emotions each item brought to me. Of the eight items, three of them I knew Bobby's grandfather either owned or experienced an event while carrying. The others belonged to various people. People I didn't know but would research. They were likely related to the neighborhood residents. I'd find out soon enough as I got to know everyone. They'd find their homes one day.

I cleared my mind and took several deep breaths. Lifting the pocket watch, I waited for more visions. I needed to locate the owner. Again, the same visions came of Bobby's grandfather and the dark-haired man. The latter held the watch, checking it again and again. I set it down. *No way around it. I'll have to ask Bobby.* I glanced at the rest of the items. *I need to meet more neighbors if these little trinkets have any hope of going home.*

A loud knock on the front door echoed upstairs. I ran down and opened it, hoping it would be Mitch. A thin, short man wearing a solemn face stood before me. He was shorter than my five feet four inches, and I had to dip my head to see his eyes under the edge of the hat he wore. His tailored suit shouted money.

"Can I help you?" I asked.

"Are you Shannon Pryce, descendent of Brenda Chambers?"

"Yes." Should I have answered that?

He handed me a folded paper. I took it and unfolded it to read.

"You've been served." He spun on his heels and ran toward the street.

I stared at him running at full throttle in his three-piece suit and brown leather shoes. His hat stayed on the entire time. His arms pumped at his sides as he jumped into a car and sped off down the street.

I locked the front door and headed to my office. I sat down. My hands shook, and I dropped the paper. Court? My heart beat against my ribs, and a loud buzz rang in my ears.

"Shan!"

Steph? She was here? Why had the lights dimmed?

I opened my eyes to see Harmony staring at me. I reached out to her. *Wait a minute*. I was on the floor. Why was I on...? *Damn, I'd passed out*. My stomach clenched, and a pain spread against the side of my head. Yep, floor and skull met. *Ouch*.

"About time," Steph said. "Good thing you were breathing or your front door would've been flapping in the breeze faster than a speeding ghost."

"What?"

"The winds would have whipped with my attempts to get someone here to help you."

"Oh." I sat up and rubbed the now throbbing bump on my left temple. "You were here when I passed out."

"Yes," she said.

"Then why'd you let me hit the floor? I've got a bump now and it hurts."

"I can't work that fast. You hit the floor before I realized you lost consciousness."

I grabbed the chair and slid onto the seat, rubbing my head. "I thought ghosts were fast."

"What are you going to do?" Steph asked.

"Get an ice pack for my head."

"Shan."

"I don't know. I guess I have to find a lawyer... A cheap lawyer."

Steph floated over to the desk, and the court papers lifted. "Who is this Lisa Parker, and how can she claim another will exists? That was what...over five years ago. Isn't that too long to contest a will?"

"How do I know? That's why I need a lawyer."

"What are you going to do about Mitch?"

I ignored her, and after she set the papers back down, I scanned them again.

"Shan."

"I know. I'm going to go talk to him in a minute. My head hurts, so give me a break. The court date is three months away, so it's not like I have to run right out and get something done."

"No need to be snippy," she said as she faded out.

Right. Whatever. I grabbed an ice pack out of the freezer and pressed it against my temple. The throbbing eased as I leaned against the counter. How did another will show up? This Lisa Parker had to be related to Aunt Caroline, but how? Was this her granddaughter she wrote about in her diary? After all this time, now she wanted the store? More questions...again.

I tossed the ice pack back in the freezer and washed up. After checking on Harmony, who had decided my laptop would be a great bed, I headed back to the office. I slipped on my gloves and after pulling out the diary, I flipped through the pages looking for any mention of a Lisa Parker. After an hour, I found the entry and quickly scanned it. So, Lisa was Beth's daughter, the girl Caroline had said *didn't* want Trinkets. But now she did?

My headache eased, and my stomach announced its need for food…again. I rubbed my belly. *You're as bad as the cat.* I headed out and across the street. Mitch and I would talk, regardless if it caused a scene or not. I hated to do that to him, but these were desperate times.

Mitch exited the diner front door with three plates in his hands. He paused when I arrived, but then turned to deliver the food. I weaved in and out of the tables and chairs to stand next to him.

"I need to talk to you," I whispered.

"I'm serving here," he responded and set a plate of fruit in front of a small elderly woman.

I nodded at the customer and smiled. Grabbing the second plate which held muffins, I put it in the center of the table. Mitch cast a look my way and set his third plate in front of the woman's companion. The gentleman smiled at us both.

106

"Is there anything else I can get you?" Mitch asked them.

I smiled at both the customers.

They both shook their heads.

"Just holler for Kim if you need anything else," he advised.

I tugged on Mitch's arm. He held back a moment then followed.

He stopped at the edge of the dining area near the street and dipped his head to whisper, "Shannon, not here. If you need to talk, I'll come around back later tonight."

"Please, I need to talk to you now. I don't want a scene either. I wouldn't do this if it wasn't urgent. You should know that." *Please, let him know that.*

Mitch scanned the diners, several of whom stared blatantly at us, but shifted their gazes quickly. He turned back to face me and sighed. "I guess what's done is done." He grabbed my arm, and we headed toward Trinkets. "Let's go."

I exhaled and led him in and up the stairs to my office.

"I've been served," I said and handed him the document I'd received earlier. I held my breath while he read. When he flipped back to the first page and started reading again, my breath whooshed out and I stood. "Well?"

"Give me a minute here."

I paced while he read the documents two more times.

"How come he has to read it three times?" Steph whispered in my ear.

I jerked and scowled at her. I tipped my head toward the door and mouthed *out*.

She grinned and shook her head, refusing.

Great. I crossed my arms, and with pinched lips, tipped my head again. Slowly, she shook her. Again. *Dang her*.

"What are you scowling at?" Mitch asked.

"You reading that three times?" I moved closer to him. "What do you think?"

"You're going to need a lawyer."

"Great. I can't afford a lawyer. Do you know who this Lisa Parker is? I know Aunt Caroline had a daughter named Beth." *Maybe I should tell him what the diary said.*

Mitch nodded. "My father told me about Beth. She went away to teach at the deaf school she attended. I think I remember seeing a girl over at Trinkets with Ms. Caroline. But the girl wasn't social, and I was hanging out with my cousins most of the time when I wasn't in school."

"I think Aunt Caroline would have been too old to have another child, don't you?"

"Well, rumor had it that the child was Ms. Caroline's from a love affair."

"What?" *What?*

"At least that's what I heard my mom gossiping about when I was home." Mitch chuckled, then pulled me in his arms. "I'm sorry about before. I shouldn't have acted like that. I'm not normally a jealous guy. I hope you understand."

"I do, but giving me the silent treatment afterwards was a bit over the top. Besides, we're talking about Bobby here."

"I tend to crawl back to my cave when things like that happen. Especially when it happens publicly. I'm working on it." He kissed my temple, then trailed to my ear. "Forgive me?"

"You want to tell me what Nancy's problem is with me? I figured she was an ex of yours, but..." I needed to know before his lips distracted me too much.

Out of the corner of my eye, Steph yawned and faded out. *Good.*

Mitch dropped his arms and paced a few steps before speaking again.

"I was engaged several years ago. It was someone I met while visiting my cousins. Well, she came for a visit and decided Petrie wasn't for her. She broke off the engagement." He gazed at me. "I'm not going to lie. I started drinking, and one night, I drank too much. I woke up that one time...*one* time in Nancy's bed. Ever since then, she thinks I'm hers."

He stared out the window. "I've explained everything to her and apologized more than once." He shook his head. "She says she understands and has been pretty good about it." He turned and wrapped his arms around me. "Until you came to town."

"And she knows how you feel about public displays."

"Unfortunately. She'll calm down soon enough once she realizes she's wasting her time."

"She will?"

He dropped a kiss on my neck and whispered, "She will."

I shuddered when his lips trailed along my ear and to my lips. A sudden buzzing pulled us apart.

He frowned and punched on his phone. After saying a few words, he hung up. "It's the diner. There's a problem with one of the customers. I need to go straighten it out. Can I come back tonight after I close?"

Was it too soon? *Nah.* I smiled and nodded.

He grabbed me for a quick, hard kiss and left.

Chapter Seventeen

After lunch, I snagged the pocket watch and marched to the pawnshop. Bobby had to recognize this watch. I pushed through the glass doors and paused, letting my eyes adjust to the lighting. Maybe Bobby thought keeping it dim would hide defects in the merchandise? I didn't see him behind the counter, but he'd know I was here by looking at his security monitors.

Walking toward the counter, I pulled out the watch, laid it on the clear glass, and waited.

"Be right there!" Bobby's sleazy voice yelled from the back.

I rolled my eyes. Must be his sales voice.

As soon as he entered the store, he grinned. "Hey, Shannon." He frowned. "You're not here to pawn something already, are you? If you need a loan..." His voice trailed off, and a flush creeped up his neck.

Oh lord. "No, no. I'm fine. I just came over to have you look at this watch again."

Bobby sidled up and pulled the watch closer, popping it open. He studied it for a moment and put it back. "Nope, I don't recognize it."

"But...it was with your grandfather's money clip. Like maybe he used it to play poker with?"

Bobby's eyes narrowed. "I don't know why he'd have that. He had his own, and I got it right here." He pulled a chain from his too tight knit pants, dangling the watch for two seconds, then he shoved it back in his pocket. It looked very similar to the one on the counter.

"Well, where would he have gotten it? Maybe a good friend of his had to pawn it?"

"Might be. But most of the time I was with my grandfather while we worked in here. I'm not sure if I could name all his friends." He chuckled.

I pursed my lips. "Shoot."

The bell over the doors jangled, and Nancy walked in, grinning. "Well, well, well. Getting some private time, huh?"

"Nancy," Bobby admonished.

I ignored her and waited. I needed Bobby's help.

Nancy sauntered next to me then stiffened. She pointed to the watch lying on the counter. "Where did that come from?" she demanded.

I jerked back. "What?"

Nancy spun on me. "I said where did that come from? That's my granddaddy's watch, you little bitch. Tell me where you got it! I'll get Rick here and make you talk. I knew there was something off about you."

Something off about me? My spine stiffened. Oh, heck no.

Bobby rushed around the counter and pulled her away from me. "Hold up there, Nancy. Shannon only came in to ask for directions. That watch there is mine. I just bought it off some scumbag from the city."

Nancy planted her fists on her hips. "You're covering for her. Some pretty little blonde comes to town, and you'd do anything to get on her good side."

Bobby straightened to his full five foot eight inches and stepped closer until there was a small gap between him and Nancy. "I told you where I got it." He held up his hand when she opened her mouth. "Stop for a minute before you make a fool of yourself. Your granddaddy's been dead for nearly twenty years now. And unless

114

Shannon lived here while she was a baby, she couldn't have anything to do with that watch."

Nancy's shoulders dropped. Her eyes filled with tears as she reached out with trembling fingers to touch the watch. "He promised to will this to me," she whispered, then sniffed. "Momma said Pappy lied. She said Pappy sold it for booze money. I believed her." She shuddered, then cleared her throat. "May I have it back, please? I'll pay you."

"You won't pay me anything. You take this," he said, handing the watch to her. "And don't tell your momma it was found. That way she can't take it away from you. You hear me?"

"I do."

Bobby patted her hand. "You know how things get misunderstood around here. I won't say anything about this if you don't."

Nancy's hair bounced as she nodded. "I won't. I promise." Her hands clasped around the watch, and she held it to her chest.

"Okay, now go on home and have a cup of tea and calm yourself," Bobby suggested.

The door's bell jangled again as she shuffled out.

I turned to Bobby. "You didn't have to do that."

"Yes, I did," he said and moved behind the counter again. "I felt bad for her seeing you and Mitch. She's always been a nice girl, just sometimes wants too much too soon. It don't help that her momma has always been a man hater."

"Thank you."

Bobby grinned. "Sure thing, sweetie. This way, you have more time to look for my stuff, right?"

I laughed and shook my head. "Right. I'll catch you later. And don't call me sweetie, Bobby," I hollered over my shoulder as I left.

His laughter followed me out into the afternoon.

Later that night, I waited by the back door for Mitch, wearing a dark purple cotton shift dress. The doorbell rang its banging song and I giggled. I hadn't told him I'd rewired it again. It was loud, but I had to keep it. I opened the door to a smiling Mitch. I'd missed his eyes and his smile.

"Hello, you," he said, his voice soft and sweet and warming me inside and out.

I moved back to allow him to enter. As soon as he stepped over the threshold, I shut the door, grabbed his shoulders, and pushed him against the door. Pressing my body hard against him, I reached up and nipped his lip, then followed it with a lick. His arms circled around me and pulled me tighter into him as he moaned.

"God, I missed you," he mumbled against my mouth.

I slipped my tongue inside his mouth and danced an erotic dance with his tongue. We both pulled away, catching our breaths, and I grabbed his curls, holding on. Our lips entwined again while he pushed the sleeves of my dress over my shoulders, and it dropped to the ground.

We kissed feverishly, and I dropped my hands, unbuttoning his shirt to reach in and stroke his chest. He bent slightly, grabbing my butt and hauling my hips up. I wrapped my legs around him, kissing his chin and cheeks. *More.* I wiggled in his embrace and he growled.

He climbed the stairs to my room and dropped me on the bed. Before the air cooled my skin, he fell atop me and pressed me down. The heat scorched my senses, and I ached for his touch. Into the night, we gave into our desires for each other.

****

Sherrie Lea Morgan

I opened my eyes as the morning sunrise splashed colors over our naked bodies. His body would make any woman ache with longing over his bulging, defined muscles. Although sore, I wanted him again. I leaned over to sneak a lick of his chin when he opened his eyes. Those chocolate-colored eyes of his. I could fall into them forever.

He grinned, showing off white, straight teeth.

"Go on. I won't tell," he whispered, then gave me a secretive smile.

So I did.

Epilogue

S teph and I stood staring at the box of trinkets on my desk. It'd been over three weeks since I moved to Petrie's Crossing, and I still hadn't met everyone in this small fishbowl town.

"It mattered," Steph whispered, although only she and I stood alone in my little office. Harmony had left hours ago.

"This time. Yes, it did."

"This time?"

"Once I start getting to know everyone, the closer I become to them, then the possibility of stronger visions will occur."

"So?"

"I don't know if I can do that. Especially with a court date and this Lisa Parker will thing looming over my head."

"Shan."

"I've already had some nightmares return. If they all come back… I don't know if I can handle it."

"You have to deal with them sometime."

"I thought I was done," I said. I walked away from the desk and stared out the window. "I've started over here. I don't want to ruin it."

"You won't. I won't let you," she said.

"You couldn't stop it before."

"I wasn't meant to stop it." Her silhouette faded then returned. "I can't stop the nightmares. I can only help you through them. Besides, this may be the way to get through it. Had you thought of that?"

"How?"

"By returning these items to their owners, you're making a difference in their lives."

"That's not a guarantee, Steph."

"No. But, it's hope."

I walked back to the desk and peered into the box, heaving a deep sigh. "Okay." I nodded and pulled the box toward me while I sat.

"Which one should I do next?" I asked.

"I really like that ring with the orange stone. You get much off of that?"

"Let me look," I said and pulled out the journal I'd made with my vision notes.

"You losing your memory? What's with the journal?"

"I decided the best way to work with this gift is to write what I've seen. Less details missed that way."

"When did you decide that?" Steph asked.

"When I started dreaming about Timmy again."

"Oh. Makes sense."

I smiled. "Yeah? Good. This time, though, I'm going to need you to do some snooping around to help me figure out the owner. I don't want to be forced to rely on Bobby or Mitch for help."

She clapped her hands. "I love snooping around."

"I know," I said, then grinned. "Let's do this."

About the Author

Sherrie Lea Morgan is an active member of Romance Writers of America and her local chapter Georgia Romance Writers. She lives north of Atlanta, GA with her twin sister, two dogs and two cats. Her goal is to encourage readers to see ghosts in a different way. When not working her current manuscripts, she enjoys spending time with her sister, daughter and son. Although her children refuse to join her paranormal movie thrills, they are supportive in her obsession of all things scary. Of course, they are always willing to travel with her.

www.sherrieleamorgan.com

https://www.facebook.com/sherrielea.morgan

https://mobile.twitter.com/slmorganwrit

40648465R00080

Made in the USA
San Bernardino, CA
26 October 2016